Walls Are to Be Walked

Walls Are to Be Walked

by NATHAN ZIMELMAN

illustrated by

DONALD CARRICK

E. P. Dutton   New York

Library of Congress Cataloging in Publication Data

Zimelman, Nathan.   Walls are to be walked.

SUMMARY: The short distance between school and home
offers an hour of adventure for a young boy.
[1. Play—Fiction] I. Carrick, Donald. II. Title
PZ7.Z57Wal [E] 77-5468 ISBN: 0-525-42175-0

Published in the United States by E. P. Dutton, a Division
of Sequoia-Elsevier Publishing Company, Inc., New York
Published simultaneously in Canada by Clarke,
Irwin & Company Limited, Toronto and Vancouver

Editor: Ann Durell
Designer: Meri Shardin
Printed in the U.S.A.   First Edition
10 9 8 7 6 5 4 3 2 1

To Sarah Zimelman
N.Z.
—————————
To Edith Blake
D.C.

Because there are swings to be swung,
And new kites have to be flown;

Because balls are not always caught
And roll and roll and roll;

Because clouds are lions,
And elephants,
And camels,
If they are watched;

Because weeds grow in Miller's lot
And spaceships can be launched
By the handful;

Because the sidewalk is rayed
By cracks
Which have to be followed
Every which-way;

Because bugs chew leaves
Very slowly,
And butterflies do not fly
In a straight line;

Because girls can not be talked to
If someone is watching;

Because lunch boxes are easy
  to forget
And have to be gone back for;

Because walls are to be walked,
And trees are to be climbed;

Because birds' nests need to be
   looked into,
And the flow of water
Is to be watched;

Because cats must be caught
Before they can be patted;

Because seven dogs have to be
visited every day;
Jimmy Jarnigan,
Age six,

Takes one hour
Walking the three blocks
From his school to his home,
Even though he runs all the way.

NATHAN ZIMELMAN says he is prompted by a memory, and then a story unfolds. With Jimmy Jarnigan's meandering journey in *Walls Are to Be Walked*, "I saw children coming home from school, and remembered how it was." Referring to the development of another book, *The Lives of My Cat Alfred*, he recalls that after the first line came to him, "It was not so much a matter of creating as of remembering."

DONALD CARRICK's home in Edgartown, Massachusetts, is three blocks from the local school. He rode his bike back and forth for a few days, prior to drawing the illustrations of Jimmy Jarnigan's walk home from school along those same three blocks. By contrast, he traveled roughly 4,000 miles to walk the desert, in preparation for his work on *Wind, Sand, and Sky* by Rebecca Caudill. He took photographs, sketched, and eventually lay still on his stomach to observe the microcosmic life. "In both cases," he said, "I discovered much I'd never seen before."

The display type is Palatino roman and the text type is Patina roman alphatype. The two-color art was prepared in watercolor. The book was printed by Rae Publishing Company.